TRACKS

David Galef

illustrated by **Tedd Arnold**

Morrow Junior Books   New York

For Daniel and Beth

—D.G.

For Rayden, Robin, and Ryean

—T.A.

Watercolors and colored pencils were used for the full-color illustrations.
The text type is 17-point Berkley Oldstyle.

Text copyright © 1996 by David Galef
Illustrations copyright © 1996 by Tedd Arnold

Printed in Hong Kong by South China Printing Company (1988) Ltd.

1 2 3 4 5 6 7 8 9 10

Library of Congress Cataloging-in-Publication Data
Galef, David.
Tracks/David Galef; illustrated by Tedd Arnold.
p. cm.
Summary: When Albert breaks his glasses while supervising the laying of the railroad tracks between two towns, he becomes responsible for one of the most exciting rides that the townspeople have ever had.
ISBN 0-688-13343-6 (trade)—ISBN 0-688-13344-4 (library)
[1. Railroads—Fiction.   2. Eyeglasses—Fiction.]   I. Arnold, Tedd, ill.   II. Title.
PZ7.G132Tr 1996   [E]—dc20   95-13264   CIP AC

In the town of Granville lived a railroad worker named Albert and his dog, Barnie. Albert had a brown mustache and a thick pair of glasses, and his job was to lay railway tracks.

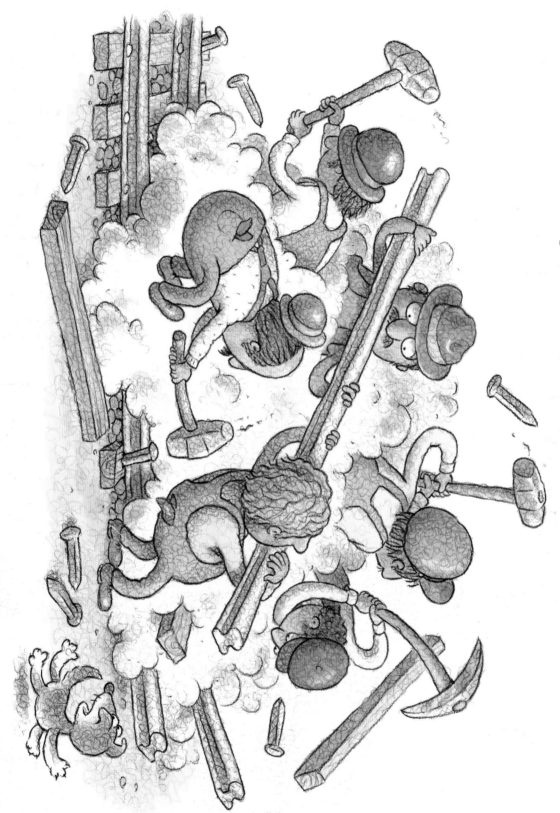

One morning, Albert and his crew were laying track for a new railroad line from Granville to Denton. Wherever Albert pointed, his crew put down the wooden railroad ties, THUD, THUD, THUD! They hammered the steel rails on top, BING, BING, BING, BING!

By noon, the new track ran straight past Henley's field and Barton's woods. But as the day grew hot, Albert's face grew sweaty. His glasses kept slipping down his nose. He kept pushing them back up. He was just bending down to pick up a railroad spike when his glasses slipped off completely. They hit a rock and broke with a *craaack*.

Albert reached for his broken glasses and put them back on. Everything around him looked blurry, but he didn't have time to go home for his other pair. Holding the glasses on with one hand, he pulled at his mustache with the other.

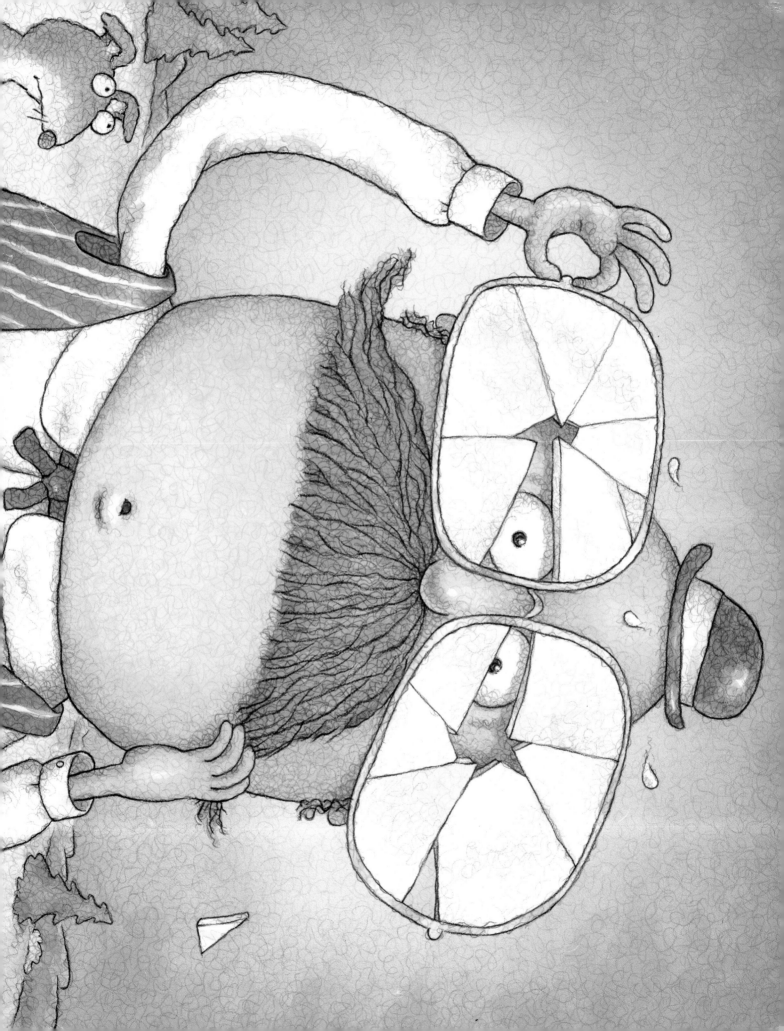

"Straight ahead!" he said, and pointed.

"Into Sally's pond?" asked one of the crew.

Albert peered ahead but couldn't see any pond, just the blue sky a little lower than usual. "I said straight!" he repeated. The men shrugged and laid the tracks through the pond, THUD, BING—*splash, quack*—THUMP!

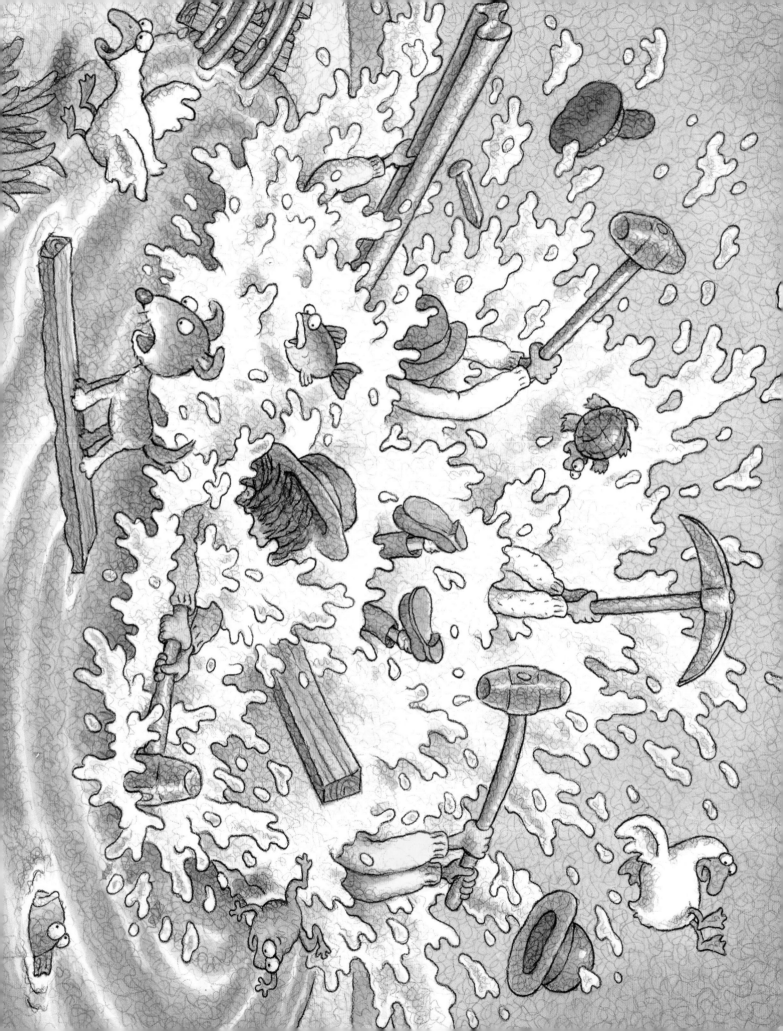

Now they were in Dunn's pasture. A herd of cows was grazing, but to Albert they looked like gray and white boulders. "We must go around these large rocks," he announced.

"What rocks?" asked one of the men.

"Don't ask questions," replied Albert. So the crew laid the tracks around the cows. But whenever the cows moved, the crew had to curve the tracks again—THUD, BING, *moo!* The track zigzagged all over the pasture, leaving a circle with cows inside.

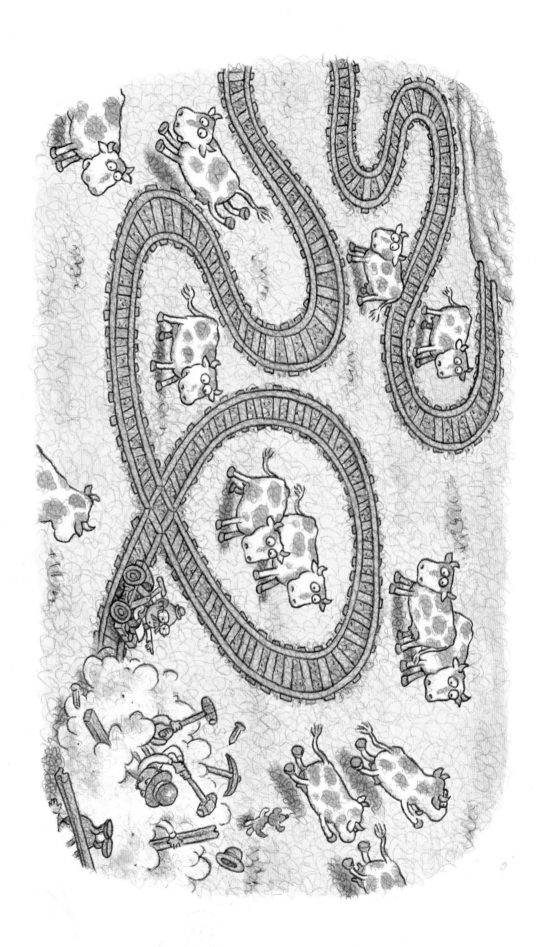

Soon they came to Calder's big red barn. To Albert, the barn looked like the red hills east of Granville. "No more detours!" he declared. "We're tunneling right through!" So the crew laid tracks straight into the barn, between the horse stalls, and out the back door: THUD, THUD—*neigh*—BING, BAM!

Next came a giant grove of pine trees. Albert pulled at his mustache. He saw a fuzzy green mountain. "We've got to go over this one!" he ordered. So his crew went up one sloping set of branches and down another: THUD, BING, *cheep*, THUD, WHAM!

They arrived in Denton late in the evening. "We've done it!" he told his crew. "Tomorrow the train will run from Granville to Denton!"

The next day, the mayor opened the new railroad line. Albert was wearing his other pair of glasses, a clean shirt, and his new straw hat. "Let us thank Albert and his crew," said the mayor. "They made this railroad line possible!" The crowd cheered.

A bunch of Granville citizens climbed aboard. The mayor got into the cab of the locomotive with Sam the engineer. Albert sat on the porch of the caboose.

The train headed straight out of town, CHUFFA-CHUFFA-CHUFFA-CHUFF. Suddenly a huge splash drenched everybody as the train ran through Sally's pond. "*Quack, quack!*" complained a duck. "*Pthew!*" said Sam as he spat out a mouthful of water.

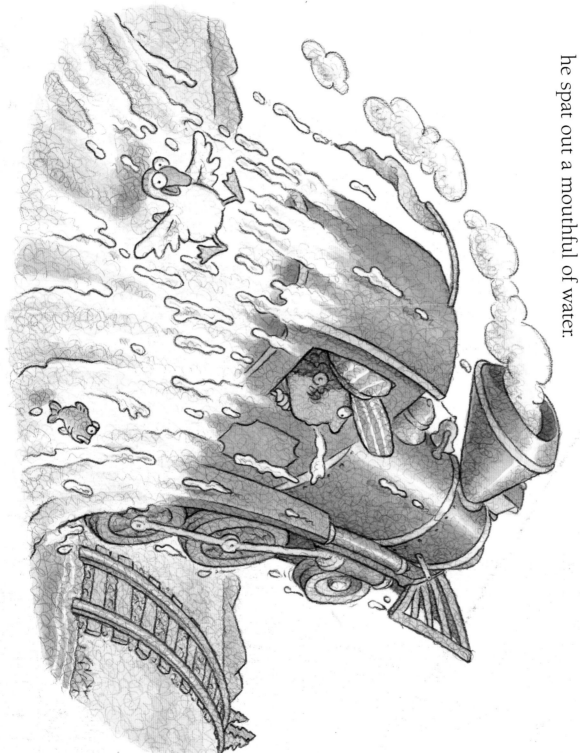

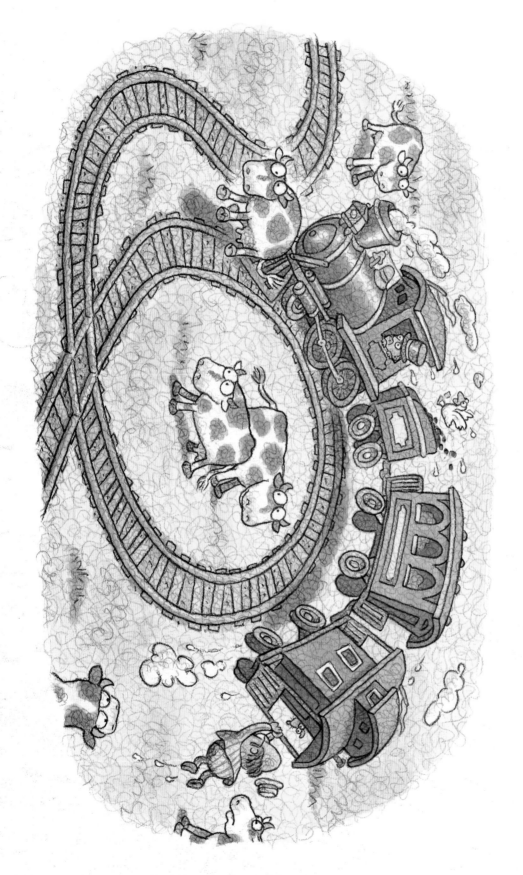

The passengers were still drying off when the train entered Dunn's pasture—and jerked to the left. All the passengers on the left side were thrown to the right. "Hang on!" yelled Sam as the train jerked to the right. Everyone was thrown to the left. "Mooo," said the cows as the train zigzagged, circled, and finally ran straight again.

Albert was leaning over the side, to see what was going on, when everything went dark. He heard a loud *neigh* as his straw hat was snatched off. When he looked back, he saw a horse chewing on it! The train roared out of Calder's barn in a cloud of hay.

"Watch out for low-flying branches!" cried Sam as the train went up into the pine trees. A nestful of robins cried, *"Cheep cheep!"* and a squirrel ran into Sam's cab.

The train climbed higher and higher till it reached the top of one huge old pine, then ran down the other side of the woods with blinding speed. It was headed straight for Denton.

When the train pulled into the station, the passengers were slow to get off. Albert just sat in the caboose, pulling at his mustache. He was very, very worried.

The first passenger off the train was an elderly man. He walked slowly past Albert. "Got to catch my breath," he said. Albert bit his lip.

The second passenger was a girl with red hair. "That was really wild!" she exclaimed. Albert swallowed hard.

Sam stepped down from the cab, shaking his head. "I've driven on a lot of railroad lines, but this one beats them all!"

"I guess it does," said Albert.

Then the mayor of Granville got out. Albert pulled at his mustache so hard it hurt.

But the mayor reached up to shake Albert's hand. "I just want to thank you for the most exciting ride I've ever taken!" he said. The crowd around the train clapped and cheered. "I haven't had so much fun in years!" the mayor went on. "I don't see how you ever got the idea for those tracks."

Albert took off his glasses to wipe his face. Everything turned blurry again. He put the glasses back on, carefully. "Well, I don't really see too well, either," he told the mayor, "but I think I will from now on."

ALBERT'S AMUSEMENT RIDES

TICKETS